GW01018305

4 Stories

The Cricket and the Mole
The Goose Opera
Jack the Lion
Robinson Hare

British Library Cataloguing in Publication Data

Janosch
  Little cricket, play for me.
  Rn: Horst Eckert I. Title II. Liebe
  Grille spiel mir was. *English*
  833'.914[J] PZ7

ISBN 0-86264-043-1

First published in Great Britain in 1983 by
Andersen Press Ltd., 19-21 Conway Street, London W.1.
Published in Australia by
Hutchinson Group (Australia) Pty. Ltd., Richmond, Victoria
3121.

Janosch.

The Cricket and the Mole
and other stories

Translated by Anthea Bell

Andersen Press · London
Hutchinson of Australia

The Cricket and the Mole

Once there was a cricket who had done
nothing all summer but play her fiddle.
She played and played and played...

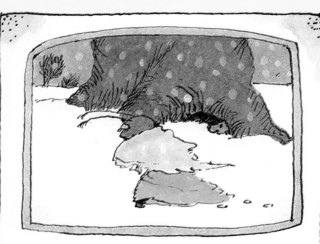

...and when winter came she had nothing to eat. She had not sown any seeds in the ground, so she had no harvest. She had not picked any wool, so she had no gloves to wear. She had not built herself a house for the winter, so she had no stove to keep her warm, and she was *freezing* cold.

So she went to see the stag beetle. "You have such fine

antlers that you must be the Head Forester of these woods," she said. "Could I come and live with you for a little while?" "Dear me, no!" said the stag beetle. "No, certainly not!"

So the cricket went away, and
went to see the mouse. She asked
if she could spare a few nuts.
"Oh, dear me, no!" said the
mouse. "No, certainly not!"

Then the cricket trudged on
again, through the bitter cold,
and she went to see the mole,
who lived in a little burrow
with a nice warm stove.

9

"A visitor, eh?" said the
mole. "Come and let me
feel you. I'm blind, so I
don't see so well. It comes
of all the black earth I
dig, but never mind."

"Oh, do stay with me!"
said the mole. "Stay and
play me something on your
fiddle, please do!"
So the cricket stayed,
and they lived happily
together in the warm.

They cooked delicious
cabbage soup with
mouse bacon for their
suppers, or sometimes
two sweet juicy peas
each.

In the evenings they
read the Woodland News
together, the stove rumbled
away, the sofa was soft
and comfortable, and
they never ...

never, never quarrelled.

What a lovely time they had! They had never been so happy in all their lives before.

The Goose Opera

*The tale of the fox
and the geese
and the warm
fur coat...*

There was once an old fox living in the woods who wanted to eat roast goose. "I'll have to go all the way to the village to catch myself a goose," said he, "for there's an old country proverb saying: If you want a goose to eat, you must be nimble on your feet."

He put on his fine yellow jacket, his plus-fours, and his hat with the feather in it, and hid his tail inside his trousers so that no one would recognize him. For there's another old proverb saying, "If once you spot the fox's tail, then run away without any fail."

Before he reached the village he heard the geese in the meadow, cackling and complaining:

"Goosey goosey gander
whither do we wander?
Out of doors in the cold
while the frost grows stronger.
The north wind doth blow, and we shall have snow,
and what will the goosey do then, poor thing?"

The old fox's mouth watered at the sight of the geese. He wanted to eat them all, but he went up to them in a friendly way.

'Oh, you poor cold geese, you're freezing!" said that wicked fox. "Maybe I can help you! I'll warm you up so well you'll never feel the cold again."

But the geese recognized him even without
his tail showing, and they cackled more
miserably than ever. They asked him to let
them sing for a while before they died, and
perform a little opera or play a singing game:

"Eeny meeny miny mo,
catch a foxy by the toe!
If he hollers let him go,
eeny meeny miny mo!
O–U–T spells OUT,
so out you go,
because the goose and gander say so!"

And the stupid fox played their game. He was It, and they chased him. He was glad they couldn't catch him, and ran so fast he was soon worn out. Then the geese played a dancing game:

"Here we come dancing with Foxy in May,
Foxy in May, Foxy in May,
here we come dancing with Foxy in May,
on a cold and frosty morning."

First one goose danced the goosestep with him, and then another, and so on. The geese did not get tired, but the wicked old fox was soon wheezing like an old tractor engine, and they could hardly keep him on his feet.

At last he toppled down and never got up again. He was dead and that was the end of him. The geese sang:

"Ring-a-ring-a-roses,
with frozen feet and noses.
A-tishoo, a-tishoo,
The fox fell down!"

They took off the fox's fine yellow jacket and his plus-fours, and stuck his handsome walking-stick deep into the ground. They left the hat with the feather in it lying on the grass, and dragged the fox himself back home to the village with them.

They skinned him, and used the skin to make themselves fur coats and warm scarves. Hadn't the wicked fox promised to warm them up so well they'd never feel the cold again?

As for his fine yellow jacket, they turned it into a carpet for the floor of their hutch, and they made his plus-fours into a bedside rug.

However, there was not enough fur to go round, and you will still see a great many poor little geese running about in the cold and the snow without any clothes on, shivering and freezing.

Jack the Lion

The short but
exciting story
of Jack the Lion
told in rhyme.

Jack the Lion wears a beard
and roars so loud
   to make you scared.

Jack the Lion goes out
      hunting
and comes back home
      with Daddy Bunting.

Jack the Lion sits in the
          clover.

He is thinking
          something over.

Then Jack the Lion
goes behind

the house to get it
off his mind.

Jack the Lion may be found
riding a horse the
wrong way round.

Jack the Lion,
        you can see,
likes to sleep
        up in a tree.

A lady comes
to shake him down.

She leaves her shoes
there on the ground.

Jack's shaggy mane
 is far too long...

but once it's cut
    it feels all wrong.

Jack the Lion's
          hairy knees
scare his little
          friend Louise.

Jack's pea soup is
on the simmer.

He gives it to Louise
for dinner.

Jack the Lion,
    feeling sick,
must stay in bed
    to get well quick.

Jack the Lion
        is all alone,

balancing on
        this big stone.

Robinson Hare

The tale of Robinson Hare
and the happy life he lived
on his island...
though not for long.

There was once a little hare who was always in trouble with his father. Father Hare spoke roughly to him, and sometimes shouted.

So one day the little hare said, "Tomorrow I'm going to pack up all my belongings in a bundle and run away to sea."

He took some hay to eat on his journey, and a couple of carrots.

The *Saucy Molly* was lying at anchor in the harbour, and a fine ship she was, all loaded up with a cargo of cabbages.

And her captain was a bold seafaring hare,
a real old salt! "Take the tiller, Able Seaman
Hare," said he. "We're putting straight out to
sea, so haul away!"

"Aye, aye, sir!" said the little hare.

He took the tiller, and the *Saucy Molly* put out to sea.

But soon the *Brave Bonaparte* hove in sight! She was a rakish pirate ship, crammed as full as she could be with buccaneering seadogs who feared neither the devil nor the deep blue sea.

They fought to the last man, until they were all dead and they sank to the bottom of the sea.

Except for the little hare, who escaped in a lifeboat and came ashore on a desert island.

He hadn't slept for seven nights, nor eaten
so much as a blade of grass . . .

. . . so he went to sleep, but when he woke
the sea had swept his boat away!

Poor little hare!

The little hare built himself a comfortable
hut, with a nice soft bed inside it.

He picked grass and herbs to eat, and lived on them.

He wove an umbrella out of leaves and wore a hat, to protect him from the wind and sun. He often went for walks on the beach, and he lived there very happily, with nobody to shout at him.

Once he saw some little wild goats playing.
He caught one and took it back to his hut,
because he had always liked his mother's
bread and milk. Yum, yum!

Then, one day, he heard pitiful weeping
and wailing in the bushes.

It was another hare, with his foot caught in a trap.

A hare just like himself, with long ears, and fur . . . only *this hare's fur was black*!

When Robinson Hare had set him free the

other hare fell at his feet in gratitude, crying, "Miha nayha misfri dey!"

Which is desert-island language and means, "I will be your friend and servant."

But what Robinson Hare thought he heard was, "My name is Friday." So he called his new friend Hare Friday.

Hare Friday carried his umbrella for him
now, picked grass and herbs, and swept out
the hut.

He cooked their meals, and caught a
cricket that would sing for them and be their
pet canary. They took a little mouse out as
their hound . . .

. . . when they went hunting, and the kind goat gave them her milk. They led a happy life there, a life as sweet as wild honey! If only it could have lasted for ever . . .

But one day a strange merchant vessel put in at the island, looking for food to take on board.

The little hare ran away, but the sailors caught him. At first they did not recognize him as another hare like themselves, because he wore so few clothes, and had grown a beard, and his fur was tanned with the sun.

But then they took him back to his father.

"Goodbye, dear island," said the hare, "goodbye, little goat and my friend Hare Friday, goodbye and farewell for ever!"

janosch.

HEY PRESTO! YOU'RE A BEAR

"A glorious fantasy picture book for every child under five who has believed his father to be invincible. Witty, amusing and wholly child-centred, a superb picture book not to be missed." *Junior Bookshelf*

THE BIG JANOSCH BOOK OF FUN AND VERSE

"A lively, idiosyncratic bundle of nursery ditties, strip adventures and mini-stories all decked with energetically expressive wash and line pictures: a box of delights for the very young to rustle through." *Growing Point*

"The nursery book of the season." *Observer*

ANIMAL ANTICS

Another large format anthology of comic animal stories, fables and verses with Janosch's lovable animal characters on every page. This is the entrancing sequel to *The Big Janosch Book of Fun and Verse*, of which the *Guardian* said: "This bumper anthology of stories and verse is outstanding—funny, lively, witty, and original, as well as being interesting enough to look at and read again and again."